First published 2000 in *The Macmillan Treasury of Nursery Stories*
This collection first published 2010 by Macmillan Children's Books
This edition published 2012 by Macmillan Children's Books
a division of Macmillan Publishers Limited
20 New Wharf Road, London N1 9RR
Basingstoke and Oxford
Associated companies throughout the world
www.panmacmillan.com

ISBN: 978-1-4472-1911-8

MACMILLAN CHILDREN'S BOOKS

The Three Little Pigs

and other stories

Retold by
Mary Hoffman

Illustrated by
Anna Currey

The Three Little Pigs

There was once an old mother pig who had three piglets. Food was short in their home so, as soon as the three little pigs were old enough, they packed some lunch into their red spotted handkerchiefs and set off to seek their fortune.

The three pigs walked down the road together and met a man carrying a load of straw.

"This is my chance," said the first little pig. "Please give me that straw and I shall build myself a house."

The man gave the pig his straw and the pig built

himself a cosy little house of straw, while his brothers went on their way, still seeking their fortune.

No sooner had the first pig settled himself snugly in his straw house than along came the big bad wolf. He peered through the tiny gap in the straw that the pig had left for a window and saw the chance of a nice dinner for himself.

"Little pig, little pig, let me come in," said the wolf.

"No, no, not by the hairs on my chinny-chin-chin," squeaked the terrified pig. "I'll not let you in."

"Then I'll huff and I'll puff and I'll BLOW YOUR HOUSE DOWN!" said the wolf, and he was as good as his word.

He huffed and he puffed and he blew the straw house right down and gobbled the little pig all up.

As the two other little pigs walked along the road, they met a man carrying a large bundle of twigs.

"Aha," said the second little pig. "This is where I get my chance. Please give me those twigs and I shall build myself a house."

And the man gave him the twigs, while the third little pig carried on seeking his fortune.

The second pig built a house of twigs, which were much stronger than straw. But as soon as he was inside it, there was the eye of the big bad wolf peeping through a space between two twigs and spying on him.

"Little pig, little pig, let me come in," he said.

"No, no, not by the hairs on my chinny-chin-chin," squealed the pig. "I'll not let you in."

"Then I'll huff and I'll puff and I'll BLOW YOUR HOUSE DOWN!" said the wolf, and he was as good as his word.

He huffed and he puffed and he blew the twig house right down and gobbled the little pig all up.

The third pig walked cheerfully along the road, all by himself, until he met a man pushing a barrow full of bricks.

"Please will you give me those bricks, so that I can build a house for myself?" asked the little pig, and the man handed them over.

The pig built himself a really strong house out of bricks, with proper windows and a door and even a chimney. He sat down by his fire and then saw something outside his window. It was the big bad wolf.

"Little pig, little pig, let me come in," said the wolf.

"No, no, not by the hairs on my chinny-chin-chin," said the pig calmly. "I'll not let you in."

"Then I'll huff and I'll puff and I'll BLOW YOUR HOUSE DOWN!" said the wolf.

So the wolf huffed and he puffed. And he puffed and he huffed.

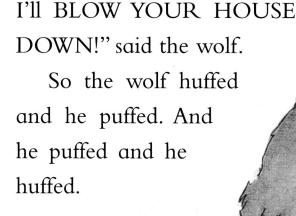

But he could not blow the brick house down.

The wolf was exhausted. And he was also furious. He was determined to eat that little pig.

So the next day he came back and said, "Little pig, I know where there is a good field of turnips."

"Where?" asked the pig.

"In Farmer Smith's field," said the wolf. "I'll take you there at six o'clock tomorrow morning."

The pig agreed but next morning he got up at five o'clock and went to Farmer Smith's field and fetched himself a nice load of turnips and was back in his house before the wolf arrived.

The wolf was very cross to have been tricked.

"Little pig," he said. "I know where there is a fine tree full of apples."

"Where?" asked the pig.

"At Merrydown," said the wolf, "and if you promise not to trick me, I'll take you there at five o'clock tomorrow morning."

The little pig agreed but next day he got up at four o'clock and went to Merrydown and climbed the apple tree. But it was further away than the turnip field and he was still up the tree when the wolf came loping along.

"What?" said the wolf. "Here before me? Are the apples nice?"

"Very nice," said the pig. "Would you like one?"

He threw an apple quite a long way from the tree and while the wolf was fetching it, the little pig ran down and back to his brick house and shut himself safely indoors.

As soon as he realised he had been tricked again, the wolf raced back to the house of bricks.

"There's a fair," he panted, "this afternoon at Shanklin. I'll come for you at three o'clock if you like."

The pig agreed but at two o'clock he made his own way to the fair. He was having a lovely time eating

toffee apples and candyfloss when he suddenly saw the wolf. Quickly, he climbed into an empty barrel and rolled down the hill towards the wolf.

The wolf was terrified as the barrel rolled faster and

faster. He jumped out of the way
and the barrel rolled to the bottom
of the hill where the little
pig's house was.
The pig ran into
his house and soon heard the wolf gasping outside.

"Oh dear, what a fright I've had! I went to the fair and
a great big round thing rolled down the hill after me and
I had to jump out of its way to save my life!"

"Ha!" said the little pig. "That was me inside a barrel!"

The wolf was so angry that he was determined to get
the little pig somehow. He started to climb onto the roof.
But the little pig guessed what he was up to and put a
great big saucepan of water to boil on his fire.

So when the wolf finally managed to squeeze
down the chimney, he fell plop into a pan of
boiling water! How he howled! The wolf
ran out of the little pig's brick house,
clutching his burnt bottom . . .
and was never
seen again.

The Gingerbread Man

Once upon a time a farmer's wife made a batch of gingerbread and with a leftover piece she shaped a little man. You might not think this unusual, because you can see gingerbread men in any baker's window, but this one was the very first such man that had ever been made.

The farmer's wife gave him raisins for eyes and, when he was baked and cooled, she took her icing bag and gave him a bow tie, a mouth and three buttons down his front.

"What a handsome fellow you are!" she exclaimed. "It will be a shame to eat you."

"Eat me!" cried the gingerbread man, sitting up on the baking tray. "No fear—I'm off!"

And he jumped off the table and ran out of the kitchen door. At first the farmer's wife was too astonished to move but, when she saw her sweet treat running away, she set off after him. But he just called out:

"Run, run, fast as you can,

You can't catch me—I'm the Gingerbread Man!"

He had soon put the farm far behind him and found himself in a village. He was running past the butcher's shop when the butcher caught sight of him.

"Stop, let me eat you," cried the butcher.

But the gingerbread man just kept running, calling back over his shoulder:

"Run, run, fast as you can,

You can't catch me—I'm the Gingerbread Man!"

He ran past the blacksmith's and the blacksmith himself came out to look. When he saw the gingerbread man, his mouth watered and he gave chase. But the little man ran on, crying:

"Run, run, fast as you can,

You can't catch me—I'm the Gingerbread Man!"

A little while later he came to the flour mill and the miller ran out to catch him. "Stop, stop!" cried the miller, "I want to eat you up!"

Well, of course, that made the gingerbread man run faster, calling out:

"Run, run, fast as you can,

You can't catch me—I'm the Gingerbread Man!"

By now he was outside the village and running across a field, where he was spotted by a very surprised cow. He nearly ran into her mouth as she munched the grass. She caught a whiff of his delicious smell and started to lumber after him, mooing in such a way that he knew what she intended.

So he ran even faster, crying out to the cow:

"Run, run, fast as you can,

You can't catch me—I'm the Gingerbread Man!"

Now he was in the horse's field and the horse came to

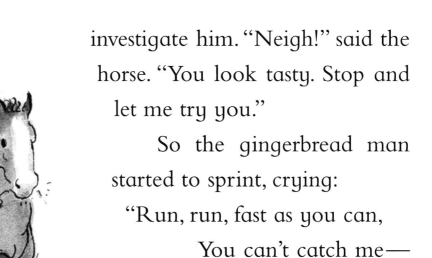

investigate him. "Neigh!" said the horse. "You look tasty. Stop and let me try you."

So the gingerbread man started to sprint, crying:
"Run, run, fast as you can,
You can't catch me—
I'm the Gingerbread Man!"

Suddenly, he realised that he could go no further. There was a stream at the bottom of the field and the horse was behind him. But there was a handsome red fox grooming himself on the bank of the stream and he offered to ferry the gingerbread man across.

The fox was the only being the gingerbread man had met that morning who hadn't wanted to eat him, so he took hold of the fox's tail and the fox started to swim across the stream. Halfway across he said to the gingerbread man, "I am afraid you will get wet. Climb onto my back." So the gingerbread man did.

Three quarters of the way across the stream, the fox said, "I am still afraid you will get wet. Why not climb onto my head?" So the gingerbread man did.

And when they were nearly at the opposite bank, the fox said, "This is the awkward bit. When I get out of the water I have to shake my fur. If you climb onto my nose you will stay dry."

So the gingerbread man climbed onto the fox's nose.

And then the fox flipped up his long red nose, opened his big greedy mouth and swallowed the gingerbread man up in one bite!

And that was the end of the first gingerbread man. Many of them have been made and eaten since and I shouldn't wonder if you've had one yourself.

The Ugly Duckling

It was lovely warm sunny weather when the mother duck laid her eggs in a quiet place by the river. She got very bored with sitting on them, waiting for them to hatch, because she missed her friends in the farmyard.

But at last the eggshells began to crack and the little ducklings poked their heads out. "Oh, what sweet babies!" cried the duck, counting her young. "One, two, three, four, five . . . oh bother! Number six has still not hatched."

The sixth egg was much bigger than all the others and, to tell the truth, the mother duck wasn't sure that it was one of hers. Birds can be very absent-minded about that sort of thing. Still, she sat on it for a few more days and at last it, too, began to crack. And out came the ugliest duckling she had ever seen.

He was much bigger than his pretty little brothers and sisters and had dull grey feathers, while theirs were fluffy yellow and brown.

"Oh dear," thought the mother duck. "Perhaps he's a turkey?"

But the ugly duckling could swim just as well as the others. His mother led them all back down the river to the duck pond in the farmyard.

"Look, here comes another clutch of ducklings," said one of the older ducks. "As if we didn't have enough mouths to feed."

"And look at that one!" said another. "That's the ugliest duckling I've ever seen!" One by one all the ducks in the farmyard noticed the new duckling. And all the hens noticed him. And all the turkeys. And they all said how ugly he was. The poor duckling felt very lonely. The girl who fed the birds was mean to him and tried to kick him. And even his own brothers and sisters teased him and called him names.

So the ugly duckling swam away from the farm along the river and found his own pond. He had no one to talk to, but one day he saw a flock of beautiful white birds flying in the sky. He didn't know what they were but his heart yearned towards them.

"Oh, how lovely to fly free with those beautiful birds," he thought. And he felt very sorry for himself. But he soon felt sorrier, when the warm days of summer were followed by the frosts of autumn and the freezing snow of winter. He had to swim round and round in circles in his pond to stop it from icing over. There was very little to eat and the ugly duckling had a wretched time of it.

Finally the spring came. The flowers started to bloom and fill the air with their scent, and the ugly duckling felt hopeful again. His wings were big and strong now and he started to fly. He flew and flew until he came to a beautiful garden full of flowers with a stream running through it.

The ugly duckling landed in the water and then around the corner came three of the beautiful white birds he had seen the year before.

"I will join them," thought the ugly duckling, "though I'm sure they will jeer at me like all the other birds."

But they didn't. They were three swans and they greeted the ugly duckling like a long-lost brother. He was so shy he lowered his head—and then he saw his own reflection in the water. He wasn't a duck at all— he was a swan!

Some children in the garden saw him and called out, "Look, there's a new swan! And he's much the handsomest."

They threw bread and cake crumbs into the water and made sure the new swan got plenty. The bird who used to be an ugly duckling was so happy. He had gone from being teased and bullied to being the handsomest swan in the garden. He spread his lovely white wings and stretched his lovely white neck and then he hid his head under his wing. He couldn't believe how lucky he was.

Rumpelstiltskin

Once upon a time there was a poor miller who found himself called to do business with a king. You might have thought that would be enough for him, but no, he had to start boasting, so that the king would think he was someone important.

"I have a daughter," he said, which was true enough. "And she is remarkably beautiful," he said, which was also true. But then he added, "And she has this gift, that she can spin straw into gold."

Oh, foolish miller! Why didn't he stop after saying he

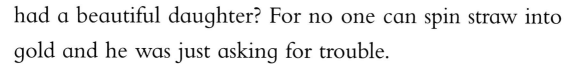

had a beautiful daughter? For no one can spin straw into gold and he was just asking for trouble.

"Really?" said the king, raising his eyebrows and looking at the miller's dusty apron. "That is a very useful gift indeed. Bring her to me so that she may show off this skill."

Now the miller was well and truly in the soup. He wished he had kept his mouth shut, but it was too late for that. He had to bring his daughter to the palace. The king showed her into a large room full of straw, with a spinning-wheel in the middle.

"Here you are, my dear," he said, kindly. "As much straw as you like. Turn it all into gold by morning or you must die."

The poor girl didn't know what to do. She hadn't the faintest idea how to start turning straw into gold, any more than you or I do. So she sat on a bale of straw and wept.

Suddenly a funny little man appeared and asked her what was the matter.

"I have to turn all this straw into gold by morning," sobbed the girl, "or I shall die."

"Well, that's nothing to cry about," said the little man. "I can do that. But what will you give me if I do?"

The miller's daughter said she would give him her necklace and the little man agreed. The girl curled up on the straw and slept peacefully all night to the hum of the spinning-wheel, until the little man needed the bale she was lying on, because he had filled every reel with spun gold.

By dawn the little man had disappeared and the room was full of reels of gold. The king couldn't believe his eyes and the miller's daughter was mightily relieved. But, that evening, the king took her to an even bigger room with even more straw in it and gave her a spinning-wheel.

"You did so well yesterday," he said, smiling. "I'm sure you will manage to turn this lot of straw into gold, too."

The girl wasn't sure at all, until the little man appeared again. He looked at all the straw.

"What will you give me this time?" he asked.

"The ring from my finger," said the girl, taking it off. And, though it was of no great value, the little man took it and set to work. By morning the room was full of spun gold.

And was the king content? You can probably guess by now what he did. He took the miller's daughter into a barn, filled with straw from floor to ceiling, so that there was scarcely room for the spinning-wheel to be squeezed in.

"This is the last time I shall ask you, my dear," said the king. "But if you turn all this straw into gold, I shall make you my queen." (For the miller's daughter really was very pretty.) "But," added the king, "if you do not, I'm afraid the terms are as before and you will die."

The girl sat at the spinning-wheel and wept. It didn't even cheer her up to see the little man appear, for she knew she had nothing left to give him.

"What, nothing?" he asked, when she explained the situation.

"Nothing at all," she said.

"All right," said the little man. "I will do it for you, but you must promise me that, if you ever become queen, you will give me your first-born child."

So the girl promised; what else could she do? And by morning the whole barn was filled with spun gold. The king clasped her in his arms and kissed her and she was queen within a week.

It had all happened so suddenly that it seemed like a dream and she forgot all about her promise. A year after the marriage, the young queen gave birth to a healthy baby boy. She was delighted with him, like any new mother. But while she was cooing over her pretty baby, the funny little man suddenly appeared in the royal bedroom and reminded her of her promise.

She was horrified. "You can't mean it!" she cried, clutching her

precious baby son. "I shall never give him up. Think of something else."

And she offered him all the riches of her husband's kingdom—jewels, gold, carriages, houses. But the little man tapped his foot impatiently.

"What do I want with all that stuff? You know I can turn even straw into gold. I want something alive."

But when he saw how distressed the queen was, he gave her one more chance.

"I'll give you three days to guess my name. If you can't, then the child is mine." Then he vanished. The next day he was back and the queen began, "Is your name Caspar? Melchior? Balthasar . . . ?" and she worked her way through all the names in the Bible. But, by the end of the day, the little man had said no to every one.

On the second day, she tried all the weird names she could think of, like Shortshanks and Grungefoot and Lumpybottom. The little man became more and more insulted, but the queen still hadn't discovered his real name.

That night she was in despair as she rocked her baby boy. She thought she would never guess the little man's name in time. Then she heard two of her servants talking. One had been out in the forest and had come to a hut with a fire outside it.

"And dancing round the fire was a funny little man singing a song," said the servant. "It went like this:

'Today I'll brew, tomorrow bake,
Then have the princeling, no mistake.
I need no fortune nor no fame,
RUMPELSTILTSKIN is my name!'"

The queen was so excited. Next day, when the little man came, she asked, "Is your name Leonardo?"

"No," said the little man.

"Is your name Brad?"

"No, no," said the little man. "You'll never get it!"

"Then," asked the queen, "is your name . . . Rumpelstiltskin?"

"Who told you, who told you?" screamed the little man, stamping his foot on the floor in such a rage that it went right through the floorboards. He pulled at his leg so hard that he split himself in half, and that was the end of Rumpelstiltskin.